Bill the Warthog MYSTERIES

THE CASE OF THE CAMPFIRE CAPER

LEGACY PRESS®

www.LegacyPressKids.com

Read more about your favorite tusked detective

in these Bill the Warthog Mysteries:

Book 1
Full Metal Trench Coat

Book 2
Guarding the Tablets of Stone

Book 3
Attack of the Mutant Fruit

Book 4
Quest for the Temple of Truth

Book 5
The Bogus Mind Machine

Book 6
King Con

Book 7
The Case of the Campfire Caper

Bill the Warthog MYSTERIES

THE CASE OF THE CAMPFIRE CAPER

Dean A. Anderson

*To my parents, Leon and Marion Anderson,
who sent me to camp and whom I was always glad
to see when I got home.*

BILL THE WARTHOG MYSTERIES: THE CASE OF THE CAMPFIRE CAPER
©2014 by Dean Anderson, third printing
ISBN 10: 1-58411-081-3
ISBN 13: 978-1-58411-081-1
Legacy reorder# LP48307
JUVENILE FICTION/Religious/Christian/General

Legacy Press
P.O. Box 261129
San Diego, CA 92196
www.LegacyPressKids.com

Illustrator: Dave Carleson

Unless otherwise noted, Scriptures are from the *Holy Bible: New
International Version* (North American Edition), ©1973, 1978,
1984 by the International Bible Society. Used by permission of
Zondervan Bible Publishers.

Printed in the United States of America

Table Of Contents

Chapter 1

The Case of the Veering Van

BANG!

One of my teachers once said it's good to begin a story with a bang, but I think she meant start it with something exciting. I don't think she meant a real "BANG!"

This was a real "BANG!"

One of the tires had blown out on the van I was in, and we'd started weaving back and forth on the road. We could have died right there.

Oh. That's right. The same teacher who gave me the "bang" advice said you should always make sure the reader knows who's who in a story. Right now, you probably don't have a clue who I am.

OK, you know how I said, "We could have died right there?" Well, the "we" was me (Nick Sayga), my friend Bill the Warthog, the van driver Mr. Stewart, (one of the Scout leaders), and a dozen middle school Scouts.

I just joined the Scouts this year. It's a pretty cool organization. They teach you about nature, how to tie knots, and how a guy should act around others. We were on our way to camp when the tire blew.

Those of you who haven't read any of my other books might wonder why a warthog was with us on the way to camp. Or maybe you think "Warthog" is just a nickname. But Bill really is a warthog. Even if you already know who Bill is, you're probably wondering why he was going with us to camp.

You see, Bill runs a detective agency, mainly solving cases for kids, and he doesn't like to leave it. And he sometimes doesn't like to go to new places because the sight of a real live warthog walking around on his hind legs and wearing dress shoes, pants, a trench coat, and a Fedora hat confuses and disturbs strangers. But Bill's my friend, and I knew he would have a blast at camp.

"I don't know if it's such a good idea to leave the agency unmanned, Nick," Bill had said.

"It's only for a week, Bill," I argued. "What do you think your answering machine is for? It's summer. Business is slow. Why not go?"

(I didn't mention one of the reasons I knew business would probably *stay* slow while we were gone. Chris Franklin, a troublemaker and the reason for a lot of Bill's cases, was also going to Scout Camp.)

What finally convinced Bill to go was the food— not the hot dogs and s'mores cooked over the camp fire, but the food Bill would find in the woods.

"There will probably be all kinds of new weeds and vegetation at that camp of yours," Bill had said. "And ticks! Do you know how long it's been since I ate a good roasted tick?"

I didn't want to think about Bill eating ticks, but this is what finally persuaded him to go to camp, and the reason he was now in the van that was swerving back and forth.

Finally, Mr. Stewart got the van under control and pulled over to the side of the road. The van with the other campers in it pulled over to the side of the road

ahead of us when they saw what had happened. The other driver, Mr. Fonda, came over to help Mr. Stewart change the tire.

"What do you think caused the tire to blow?" Mr. Fonda asked.

"I know exactly what caused the tire to blow," Mr. Stewart said. "One of the boys in your van threw a bottle out the window, and the broken glass on the road punctured the tire."

They went to work putting on the spare tire and got us back on the road, but I knew someone was going to be in trouble at the next break.

When we pulled over at a rest area, Bill and I headed for the drinking fountains. I heard Mr. Fonda say, "I found out who threw the bottle out the window—it was Mike Green."

It just so happens that Mike is a friend of mine and Bill's. Although Mike draws a lot of crazy things in the comics he makes, he doesn't tend to do crazy things. So I felt I had to say something.

"What makes you think Mike threw the bottle out the window?" I asked. "Did you see him do it?"

"I didn't see him do it," Mr. Fonda said. "But one of the other Scouts, Chris Franklin did. Of course, Mike's

denying it, as some kids do."

Mr. Fonda and Mr. Stewart had just started working with our Scout troop. There's no way anyone who knew Chris and Mike well would take Chris' word over Mike's.

"Perhaps we could interview the boys together," Bill suggested.

"I don't think you understand how we do things in our country," Mr. Stewart said. "It is best in our country for the adults to take care of these things."

(Somehow, Mr. Stewart had gotten the idea that Bill was an exchange student. He had heard that Bill was from Africa, as are all warthogs, and I guess he thought that Bill's heritage explained his unique appearance and wardrobe choices.)

"Mr. Stewart, Bill is really good at getting to the heart of a case," I said. "You won't regret bringing him into this."

It took a little more persuading, but eventually Mr. Stewart and Mr. Fonda agreed to let Bill ask Mike and Chris some questions while the Scout Masters listened.

"Mike, what were you doing when the bottle was thrown?" Bill asked.

"I was drawing comics, Bill," Mike said. "That's usually what I'm doing when I have free time."

"Did you see who threw the bottle, Mike?" Bill asked.

"Sorry, I was just concentrating on my drawing."

"I'll tell you who threw the bottle," Chris said. "I hate to be a tattletale, but this could have been a very dangerous situation. Mike threw the bottle."

"What are you talking about?" Mike said angrily.

"Be patient, Mike," Bill said. "What were you doing when the bottle was thrown, Chris?"

"I'll tell you, Pigman…" Chris began.

"Chris," Mr. Stewart said, "Just because someone is from another country doesn't mean you can call them names."

"Um, oh, er, yeah," Chris stuttered. "Anyway, me and my friends were actually playing the alphabet license plate game."

"What is that?" Bill asked.

"You've never played that game?" I asked, amazed there was something I knew about that Bill didn't. "It's the game where you try to be the first to collect all the letters from license plates on other cars. You start with A and work through to Z."

"Exactly, Narc, I mean Nick," Chris said. "We were toward the end of the game and I saw a car with all the letters I needed: Q through Z. So I looked back to be sure it had all the letters, and I saw Mike throw the soda bottle. My friends will back me up on that."

"I guess we'll have to talk to your friends, Chris," Mr. Fonda said.

"No need, Mr. Fonda," Bill said. "I could tell Chris' story was phony from the beginning. Beginnings are important, Chris. Because we're out in nature this week, maybe you could consider the very beginning and your need to begin again."

How did Bill know Chris wasn't telling the truth? And what did Bill mean by "the very beginning"?

 Turn to page 92 to find out!

Chapter 2

The Case of the Sticky Doorknobs

The vans strained a bit driving up into the mountains. The scenery was amazing. On one side of the van was a huge forest of fir and pine trees. On the other side of the van was a very scary drop-off. I tried to look at the forest only.

Eventually, we drove beyond the drop-off and into a gorgeous valley with a lake. Mr. Stewart's promise of being "almost there" came true as we drove by a signpost reading, "Welcome to Camp Cheese Waddles!"

Back home, we'd all wondered about the camp's name. Mr. Fonda explained that the first campers were allowed to vote on the camp name, and

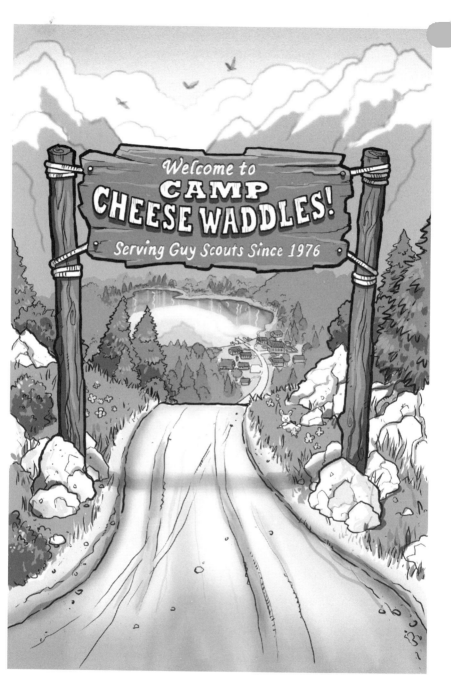

apparently their favorite snack food was Cheese Waddles. Strange name, but considering my nickname, "Ten Toes" (from my habit of playing video games with my feet), who am I to talk?

When we arrived, we saw buses and vans with kids from all over. We heard that there were almost 200 kids at camp for the week. Mike, Bill, and the rest of us guys registered at the main office. They assigned cabins to everybody, and we climbed uphill to ours. We had a great view looking down toward the lake. "How fitting," Bill exclaimed. "West Sierra Lake is west of our cabin!" Fortunately, we weren't in the same cabin as Chris Franklin and his gang, although they were in the cabin just up the hill and east of our cabin.

We went back down to the main camp for dinner. The dining hall was huge. With all the kids and counselors it was quite loud. One wall was covered with mounted deer heads. (Bill said the mounted heads always reminded him of big game hunters in Africa, but it didn't bother him enough to hurt his appetite.)

Soup was the main course for the night: beef or vegetable. Usually I'm not a big soup fan, but I was hungry and this was great soup. Even better than the soup was the bread: big, homemade, steaming hot loaves at each table. There was butter and big jars of honey for the bread. The butter and honey melted together when spread on the bread. It was so good we really didn't need dessert.

Still, I was glad for the apple pie topped with vanilla ice cream. Bill insisted on calling it *"pie a la mode,"* because he said he had so few opportunities to use his French.

After dinner, the director of the camp, Mr. Wayne, gave us a talk. He shared the camp rules (boundaries,

lights out, etc.). Then, he talked about the flora and fauna. "Plants and animals," Bill explained when he saw my puzzled look.

Mr. Wayne said that he would like for us to have fun with the games, activities, and hikes this week, but he also wanted us to enjoy the beauty of the world around us and to take time to think about what that beauty meant.

I saw Chris and some other guys rolling their eyes, but anyone would have to admit this was a really beautiful place.

Then, we were off to our cabins. I think I was asleep before the lights were out.

When I woke up the next morning, I knew I had to leave the cabin because—how should I put this—the cabin did not have certain, um, waterworks. I put on my sandals and was out the door. I used the outhouse that several of the cabins shared and then walked back to my cabin.

I put my hand on the doorknob. My hand felt sticky. I tried to wipe the sticky stuff off one hand with the other but now they were both sticky. I smelled my hands and knew someone had spread honey on the doorknob.

Out of the corner of my eye, I noticed a kid coming out of a neighboring cabin. Then I heard a scream.

I ran over to see what was wrong with the kid, and suddenly Bill and Chris bolted out to join us.

"What's wrong?" I said to the kid. I soon saw what was wrong—his foot was bleeding.

The kid was crying, "I didn't...*sniff*...see it..."

There was honey on the other cabin's doorknob, and a broken honey jar someone had dropped on the cement. The kid had stepped on the broken glass with his bare foot.

"Let's get him to the nurse," Bill said.

We learned on the way down the hill the kid's name was Ethan. He put one arm on Bill's shoulder and the other on mine. Chris ran ahead to alert the nurse.

The nurse was Mrs. Wayne, the wife of the camp's director. Both Mr. and Mrs. Wayne were waiting for us. While Mrs. Wayne tended to Ethan, Mr. Wayne spoke to the three of us.

"From what Chris tells me, you two have some explaining to do," he said.

"Oh really?" Bill said. "I'd be interested to hear Chris' story."

"OK," Chris said. "Well, I woke up early because the morning light was shining in my eyes. I looked out the window to see the lake. The sun's glare kept me from seeing too clearly when I looked down the hill, but I know I saw two figures pouring honey on doorknobs. There was no mistaking your shape, Warthog. You dropped the honey jar which led to Ethan's injury."

"Well, Mr. Wayne," Bill said. "It is only fitting that on the first day of camp, we should shed some light on Chris' character."

Mr. Wayne listened and Chris was soon in trouble with the camp director. But I couldn't figure out why until Bill explained.

How did Bill and Mr. Wayne know that Chris wasn't telling the truth? And what did Bill mean about it being "fitting that on the first day, we should shed some light on Chris' character"?

 **Turn to page 94 to find out!**

Chapter 3

The Case of the Waterskiing Warthog

On the first morning of camp, we had French toast for breakfast. I noticed that the counselors kept a close watch on the pitchers of maple syrup—probably because of the doorknob incident the night before.

After breakfast, Mr. Wayne announced that there would be sign-ups for various activities. He said it would be better to show us the activities rather than tell us about them, so a big screen came down from the ceiling.

We watched a video with kids horseback riding, waterskiing, hiking, rappelling, and rock climbing. I was blown away by all of the options.

Mr. Wayne said, "You won't have time this week to do everything and some activities will fill up quickly." He said we could sign up on the clipboards in the back once our tables were cleaned and we were excused.

The guys at our table cleaned up in record speed. We were the third table excused, and Mike and I pushed Bill straight to the table with the waterskiing sign-up. I had a picture in my mind of a warthog being pulled on skis behind a boat, and I had to see that in real life.

When we got to the table, all the ski slots for that day had already filled up, so we signed up for the

6:00 AM slot the next morning. Then we signed up for some cool things for the rest of the week—horseback riding, high diving, and rock climbing. The only activity open for that afternoon was lanyard making. I made a mighty fine lanyard that day. I also hung out at the pool and played a pick-up game of Ultimate Frisbee. Throughout the day, I was thinking about the next day's waterskiing.

That evening, I set the alarm on my watch to make sure I woke up in time but I didn't need to use it. I didn't sleep well because I was excited—and because Bill was snoring.

You might think you've heard snoring, perhaps from your dad or a brother or sister or a friend. Trust me — you have not heard snoring until you've heard a warthog snore.

A warthog snore shakes rafters and rattles windows. The only good thing it does is scare off the mosquitoes.

I woke up a little before my 5:00 AM alarm. I then woke Mike, and he helped me wake up Bill—definitely a job for two people because Bill sleeps soundly.

Mike and I put on our bathing suits and then Bill put on his. I don't know if you've ever seen pictures of people wearing bathing suits from the early 1900's, but Bill was wearing one of those. Apparently he thought suits for guys should cover you from the knees to the neck.

It was still cool outside, so we wore our sweats down to the lake. There was a speed boat at the dock, and the man by the boat introduced himself. "My name is Mr. Speed and I'll be driving your boat today."

Mr. Speed went over the rules for waterskiing. When a person was in the water, one person in the boat would always keep an eye on him and use a flag to signal to other boaters that someone was in the water.

Mr. Speed showed us how to put on the skis and how to signal if we wanted to go faster or slower or stop. Finally, it was time to ski.

Mike went first. He had skied before and only needed one ski. He got up the first time and skied for a long time until he got tired and fell.

It took me several tries to get out of the water. The first few times my skis slipped away or the boat just dragged me with my head underwater. When I finally got up, it was a blast. I even cut back and forth over the boat's wake a couple of times before I went down.

It was even tougher for Bill. The skis were built for feet, not hooves, but Mr. Speed had some extra rope and he tied Bill to the skis. Bill had to hold the tow rope's handle in his mouth.

It took several tries and increases in speed (heavier skiers sometimes need more speed to get up), but eventually Bill was skiing. Mr. Speed handed me a waterproof camera to get pictures for the camp slide show.

After skiing a bit on all fours, Bill kicked the ropes off his front feet and started skiing on just his hind legs. He crashed pretty quickly after making the switch.

Our time with Mr. Speed was up, so we went in. We dried off and headed for a breakfast of pancakes with strawberries. We sat at a table with Ethan, the honey jar victim from the day before.

"The best part of water skiing," Bill said, "is when the bugs fly in your mouth."

"I love jumping the wake and feeling the spray in my face," Mike said.

"Too bad I can't go in the water with my stitches," Ethan said. "Otherwise, I would show you some real waterskiing."

"Mike can ski on one ski," I said.

"I ski barefoot," Ethan said.

"Bill was skiing really fast," I responded.

"I ski really fast," Ethan said. "Over a hundred miles an hour."

"Really?" Bill asked. "How do you know you were going that fast?"

"Once I got back in our family's sailboat, which is worth half a million dollars," Ethan said, "Dad pointed

to the speedometer. He said, 'You were going this fast,' and pointed to the mark that read '100 MPH.'"

Throughout the rest of the meal, Ethan bragged about all the stuff his family had, how good he was in school and at sports, and all the famous people he knew.

After the meal I asked Bill if he believed all the stories Ethan told.

"His skiing story certainly didn't hold water," Bill said. "Speaking of which, I am certainly grateful for the second day."

Why didn't Bill believe Ethan's waterskiing story? And why did Bill say he was thankful for the second day?

☞ **Turn to page 96 to find out!**

The Case of the Poison Oak Sandwich

The next morning I woke up early and excited. (Bill had slept on his side, so he snored a little less and we all slept a lot better.)

I was excited because we were going on a day-long hike up to Eagle's Point with Mr. Stewart and twenty other campers. We met at the dining hall early, an hour before the rest of the camp had breakfast. We scarfed down granola bars and orange juice. We packed five backpacks with food and water which we would take turns carrying. Mr. Stewart said the hike was fifteen miles round trip so we'd better get going.

As we started up the trail, Mr. Stewart said he'd take the lead and that Bill was to follow at the back of the group. Mr. Stewart wanted us all to stick together, but we kept spreading out. Bill was trying to encourage the hikers in front of him to move along. He was using great self-restraint by not "encouraging" them with his tusks.

We could tell we weren't the first people on the trail that day. (I'd rather not tell you how we knew horses had been on the trail already that morning.) We didn't see the horses, but we did see squirrels, chipmunks, and some odd-looking creatures that Mr. Stewart said were yellow-bellied marmots. Even more amazing were the trees and the fields full of flowers in bloom. Ethan was moving very slowly. I think the stitches in his foot were bothering him. The trail started getting really steep and rocky. Ethan moved slower still.

We stopped for a break. It was getting warmer, so everyone took big gulps from their water bottles. Bill went to talk to Mr. Stewart, and they came back to talk to Ethan together.

"Our Nigerian friend here…" Mr. Stewart began.

"I'm not from Nigeria," Bill interrupted.

"Oh, sorry," Mr. Stewart said. "Our friend here from the Congo tells me you're having troubles keeping up, Ethan."

"Yeah," Ethan said. "My foot is really bothering me."

"It's just going to get tougher," Mr. Stewart said. "No shame in stopping here if you need to."

"Maybe that would be best," Ethan said.

Bill agreed to stay back with Ethan, and I said I'd stay too. Everyone else would go on to the top and eat lunch at Eagle's Peak. We'd wait for them to come back. That way Ethan would have a chance to rest up before the trip back down.

Mr. Stewart pulled out some sandwiches and fruit for us, along with a couple more water bottles. He and the other hikers left Bill, Ethan, and me sitting on some big boulders.

"Very disappointing," Bill said as he unwrapped his sandwich.

"What's wrong, Bill?" I asked.

"I asked for greens on my sandwich," Bill said. "It didn't happen."

"Let me have that sandwich," Ethan said. "I'm somewhat of a plant expert, so I can find some wild greens for your sandwich."

Ethan grabbed Bill's sandwich and went hopping on one foot into the trees. He was back a couple of minutes later, with greens creeping out of the bread.

Bill examined the sandwich. "I'm afraid, Ethan, if I eat this, I'll have an itchy mouth and stomach. I think you picked poison oak."

"No way," Ethan said. "You see, I've gone hiking just about everywhere with my dad, who's a wilderness expert. We spent a summer in the Rockies living off the land.

"We hunted for game and ate wild nuts, fruits, and berries. We did the same thing one summer in the Appalachian Mountains.

"I remember my dad clearly, both in the Rockies and the Appalachians, pointing to plants and saying, 'Stay away from that, son, it's poison oak.' I helped Dad write field guides for identifying wild plants."

"Ethan," Bill said, "I'm afraid I don't believe you are an expert on plant life. You seem to believe you need to make up stories to impress us. You don't need to make up stories to be our friend."

Ethan admitted he had been making up stories, not only then, but also the day before with his waterskiing stories. Ethan said he was afraid people wouldn't bother getting to know him if he didn't come up with tall tales about himself.

We had a good time after that, just talking and hanging out. And the stuff Ethan said after that was much more believable.

Bill didn't eat his ham and wild greens sandwich. (We confirmed with Mr. Stewart later that the "wild greens" were actually poison oak.) Ethan and I each gave him part of our sandwiches.

After lights out that night, I asked Bill how he knew Ethan wasn't being truthful.

"Something he said planted the seeds of doubt," Bill said.

"Were you disappointed we didn't go all the way up the trail?" I asked.

"It was OK," Bill said. "I didn't mind just sitting around and talking. After all, on the third day, it is appropriate to veg out."

How did Bill know that Ethan wasn't telling the truth? And why did Bill say that it was appropriate to veg out on the third day?

 Turn to page 98 to find out!

Chapter 5

The Case of the Meteor Bath

The next day, after a full morning—eating breakfast, paintball, a pick-up touch football game, some hacky-sacking, and lunch—Bill and I fell asleep in lounge chairs by the pool. Mike Green woke us up.

"Hey, guys," Mike said. "Want to look at this?"

I had been perfectly happy looking at the inside of my eyelids, but Mike's a good guy. "Sure," we said in unison.

"I've been working on a *Phil the Warthog* comic, and I wanted you guys to see it," Mike said.

"I wondered where you had been all day," Bill said. "I shouldn't be surprised."

Mike loved to draw cartoons, and he was good at it. For a while now he'd been chiefly drawing *Phil the Warthog* comics. He wouldn't admit that Phil was based on Bill, but it was pretty obvious, especially because Mike always showed his Phil comics to Bill before anyone else.

Mike laid the comics on a nearby table to show us. The first panel showed Phil talking with government agent Shady Thomkins:

• •

"So as I understand it," Phil said, "Dr. Werner von Doomcough has collected bathtubs from trash dumps around the world and plans to send them into space."

"Exactly," Shady replied in the next panel. "And he plans to drop those bathtubs back to Earth in highly populated areas during the upcoming meteor shower unless the government pays him $2 trillion and a lifetime supply of yummy Cheese Waddles."

"Something absolutely must be done to stop him," Phil replied.

"Exactly," Shady answered. "And that's why we're sending you into space!" The next panel showed Phil with an expression of surprise.

The following panels showed Phil in a space

suit boarding a rocket, and the rocket launching into space.

Phil then emerged from his ship in a space suit with a propulsion unit and navigated toward his goal: the bathtub graveyard in space. There were bathtubs as far as Phil could see.

Some of those bathtubs were chained together. Some were equipped with tiny rockets for a planned re-entry into Earth's atmosphere to rain havoc on the people of the planet.

Then Phil saw someone in a spacesuit in the distance. Phil could also see that the man was

 installing more rockets on more tubs. Phil turned his propulsion jet on high to chase the man.

The man in the spacesuit saw Phil and off he went. He flew under, above, and around the tubs. Phil saw him fly behind one of the space tubs, and Phil thought he had the spaceman trapped. But the man had just installed a rocket on the tub. He ignited it and sent it barreling toward Phil.

Phil dodged the oncoming tub, but it smashed into

the tub behind him. Since sound doesn't travel in the vacuum of space, Phil didn't hear the collision or notice the large piece of porcelain flying toward his head.

The piece of tub that hit Phil didn't tear his suit, but it did send him spinning.

The space spin proved fortunate because, as he was spinning, Phil saw another space ship in the vicinity. A vent door on the ship was still open, but it was slowly closing. Again, Phil set his propulsion jets to maximum speed and was able to enter the ship just before the vent door closed.

After decompressing in a decompression chamber, Phil made his way to the bridge of the ship. There, he saw a man in ragged clothes at the helm of the ship.

"Who are you?" the man asked.

"Phil the Warthog, Government Agent," Phil answered. "And who are you?"

"Me?" the man in the tattered shirt and pants answered, "I'm a garbage man sent up to collect all these bathtubs."

"Is there someone else on this ship?" Phil asked.

"Just me," the man answered. "I was trying to figure out how to collect all these bathtubs when I heard someone cry for help from outside the ship.

I had no idea that there was anyone out there, but when I heard the yelling, I opened the vent door."

"You're telling me you had no idea who was outside the ship?" Phil said. "And you just opened your vent door for the person when you heard a call from outside your ship?"

"Exactly," the galactic junk man said.

Phil looked the man in the eye and said, "I know you're lying. I think you're working for Dr. Werner von Doomcough. And I want to know who else you let onto your ship."

The next panel showed Dr. Werner von Doomcough himself in a space suit with a laser pointed at Phil's back.

"Excellent," the bad Doctor said. "How did you know that my friend was not telling the truth? Of course, it does not matter. Soon you will be part of the meteor and bathtub storm hurling toward planet Earth."

To Be Continued....

• •

I always hated reading "to be continued," but I knew Mike would get us the next installment soon.

"Good work," Bill said to Mike, "Though, as usual,

this tale is more than a tad unlikely. Did you get the idea for the story from tonight's activity?" (That night we were going to camp outside to watch a summer meteor shower.)

"Of course," Mike said.

"Hey Mike," I said. "How did Phil know the guy was lying?"

"That should be obvious," Bill said. "As obvious as the fact that the fourth day of camp is a wonderful time to watch a meteor shower."

How did Phil know the man was lying? And what does the fourth day have to do with a meteor shower?

 **Turn to page 100 to find out!**

Chapter 6

The Case of the Snacking Bear

If it weren't for me, we would have had the cleanest cabin in the whole camp. There were five other guys in our cabin besides Bill, Mike, and me. The other guys were picky about keeping the cabin clean.

Bill could be a slob in his office, but out of courtesy to our bunkmates, he was keeping things spic and span in his part of the cabin.

So it was kind of everyone else in the cabin to turn a blind eye to my heap of dirty clothes and my comics spread on the floor. They just insisted that I not bring food into the cabin, and on the fifth full day of camp, I was glad they insisted on it.

After breakfast, I realized that I had forgotten my sunscreen. When Bill went up to the cabin with me to get it, we heard loud rustling sounds in the cabin near ours.

We were quite surprised when we looked through the door of the other cabin. A big black bear was sitting on its hind legs in the middle of the cabin, holding a box of Cheese Waddles. The bear picked out one Waddle at a time with its paw, held each Waddle up and dropped it in his mouth.

Okay, I admit it. I screamed.

This got the bear's attention and apparently the attention of some other campers who came running up the hill.

The bear was done with the Cheese Waddles because it threw down the bag and started walking toward us.

"Walk backwards slowly and raise your hands in the air so you appear bigger than you are," Bill said perfectly calmly.

I did as Bill said. We both walked back up the hill, but the bear was still walking toward us.

I don't know if my foot hit a tree branch or a rock; I just know that I fell backwards.

I was lying on my back on the ground, and the bear was still walking toward me.

Suddenly, Bill was on all fours between me and the bear. He nodded his head up and down, like he was ready to charge with his tusks and made piercingly loud grunting sounds. The bear seemed to want no part of this; it turned and ran off into the woods.

I saw Mr. Fonda running up the hill along with a bunch of other campers.

"Did you see it?" I called to Mr. Fonda.

"I did," he called back.

By the time he reached us, I had gotten back on my feet.

"That looked like a 400-pound black bear," Mr. Fonda said. "It didn't seem to care for your tribal war cries, Bill."

"Let's see what kind of damage it did in the cabin," Bill said.

 I hadn't noticed what a mess the cabin was before because my concentration had been on the bear. Besides the empty box of Cheese Waddles, there were candy

wrappers and chip bags all over the floor. Even worse, a backpack and a couple of sleeping bags had been badly shredded by bear claws.

"Why did the bear tear those things up?" I asked Mr. Fonda.

"There was probably food in the pack and the sleeping bags," he said. "Or at least the smell of food."

Chris Franklin and a kid named Donald that I'd just met at breakfast came in the door. (At breakfast, Donald had been complaining about a bunkmate that kept calling him "The Duck." He was surprised when I guessed that his bunkmate was Chris.)

"Boys," Mr. Fonda lectured, "this is why we told you not to bring food into the cabins."

"I didn't do it," Chris piped up. "I kept telling Donald here that he shouldn't bring food in the cabins, but he wouldn't listen. To learn his lesson, he should probably do all the cleanup and pay for the sleeping bags and backpack."

"Is that true, Donald?" Mr. Fonda asked.

"No," Donald said. "Chris was the one who brought food in the cabin."

"You can be sure it wasn't me," Chris said. "And I can tell you why. Back home at our house we've had problems with animals getting into our garbage, so I'm really sensitive about it."

"I'd like to hear more about that," Bill said.

"Well," Chris said, "we haven't had a problem with wild pigs in our garbage YET. But we did have a problem with raccoons.

"Sometimes I would leave the dog food outside during the day. The dog food would be gone when I came home from school, even though my dog was inside all day."

"His dog is named Mr. Happyface," I couldn't help adding. Chris had named his dog when he was little, and now it embarrassed him.

"Anyway," Chris went on, "then we started having problems with animals getting into the garbage when no one was around. But one day, I came home early from school and saw a couple of raccoons in the garbage can.

"From then on, we left my dog on a rope outside during the day, and that scared off the raccoons. But you can see why I would be sensitive to the food and animal problem."

"But I didn't leave the food in the cabin!" Donald protested.

"It's your word against Chris'," Mr. Fonda said.

"It's not," Bill said. "May I have a word with you, Mr. Fonda?"

Bill and Mr. Fonda stepped outside.

Then Mr. Fonda gave Chris quite a talking to.

"So how did you show Mr. Fonda that Chris was lying?" I asked.

"Just a matter of animal knowledge," Bill said. "Although it would be more appropriate to talk about animals tomorrow—the sixth day of camp."

"So it was something to do with the bear?" I asked

"Oh, not the bear," Bill said, "though I have always liked bears. Did you know that the word for a group of bears is a 'sleuth'? That's also a word for a detective— such a noble creature."

How did Bill convince Mr. Fonda that Chris was lying? And why did Bill say that it would be more appropriate to talk about animals on the sixth day of camp?

 Turn to page 102 to find out!

Chapter 7

The Case of the Confident Cowgirl

First of all, let me make one thing perfectly clear: if I had known that going horseback riding involved going to Camp Buttercup, I probably wouldn't have signed up. But I didn't know that. I only knew that a good guy in our cabin, Luke Snider, wanted to go and he wanted someone to go with him.

Not only did Luke love to ride horses, he even rode in rodeos. It didn't take much convincing to get Luke to pull out his scrapbook with programs and ribbons from rodeos as well as pictures of Luke riding bucking broncos.

So Bill and I agreed to sign up for horseback riding

on Saturday, the sixth full day at camp. After we signed up, I learned we had to go across the lake to the Gal Scout Camp.

Camp Buttercup was founded the same year as Camp Cheese Waddles, (its name was also chosen by its first campers.) After breakfast, ten of us got in boats to go across the lake to the girls' camp.

We had a few minutes to look around the camp before we went to the corral. It was a nice camp, but not as good as ours. I heard, though, that the girls' cabins had indoor restrooms.

The corral was pretty impressive. There must have been fifty horses, and there were twenty campers ready to ride (10 guys and 10 girls). But first we had to get instructions from Wrangler Scott. We sat on two benches, boys on one bench and girls on the other.

I could tell Luke was a little bored with the instructions on the basics of riding. I also noticed that one of the girls kept trying to get his attention, waving and stuff.

"Who's she?" I whispered to Luke.

"Caroline Bodle, a girl from my school back home," Luke said.

"Does she like you or something?" I asked.

Luke looked disgusted and shrugged his shoulders.

After the instructions, Wrangler Scott and some of the counselors went to get the horses and equipment.

As Bill, Luke, and I were talking, Caroline came over to talk to Luke.

Luke introduced Caroline to Bill and me.

"You know," Caroline said, "I heard some of our counselors talking about you. Is Warthog some kind of tribal name?"

"Well, not exactly," Bill said. "In fact, I should point out that it is actually…"

But Caroline's attention was already back on Luke.

"I kept checking the sign-up lists to see when you might be coming over here to ride," she said. "I mean, I would have gone riding anyway because I love it. But I thought, well, it would be kind of fun if we happened to go riding on the same day."

"I didn't know that you were interested in horses," Luke said.

"Oh yeah," Caroline said. "I've been riding since I was really little. I ride in shows and stuff, riding around the barrels and such. It's a big part of my life."

"That's interesting," Luke said. "Because I…"

But before Luke could get to his rodeo stories,

Wrangler Scott asked for everyone's attention.

"Listen up, Buckaroos," Wrangler Scott said. "I have a horse here that only an experienced rider should ride. His name is Wild Fire, and he has earned that name.

"He's real fast, but he'll take over if you don't show him you're in control. So who here thinks they can handle him?"

Caroline's hand shot up.

"You think you can handle him, little lady?" Wrangler Scott asked. "He's a lot of horse."

"I'm a very experienced rider," Caroline replied confidently. "I'm sure I can handle him."

"Ok," the horseman said. "Let's get rides now for the rest of y'all."

When I told Wrangler Scott I had never ridden a horse before, he got me a horse by the name of Sweetfoot. Even though this was a little 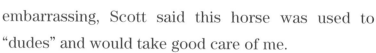 embarrassing, Scott said this horse was used to "dudes" and would take good care of me.

Wrangler Scott looked at Bill for a long time. He asked Bill's weight. Then he went into the big barn.

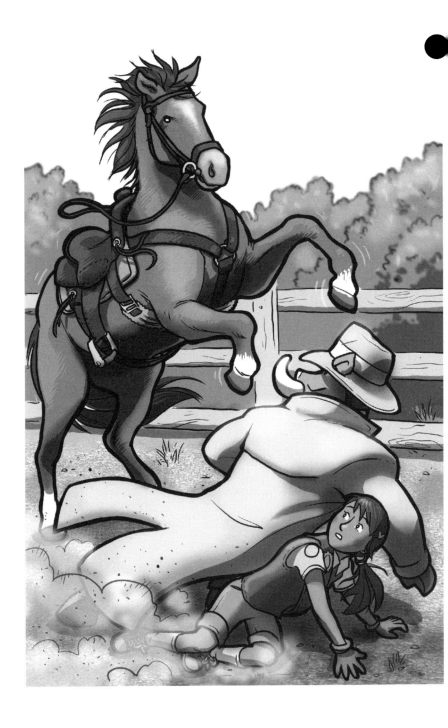

"I suppose I offer a bit of a challenge," Bill said.

Wrangler Scott came out with the biggest horse I had ever seen. It had huge white legs and the rest of its brown body was massive as well. It seemed twice the size of my horse.

"I reckon this Clydesdale will do ya," Wrangler Scott told Bill. Then he said, "Alright, time for everyone to mount up."

The more experienced riders were to mount their horses in the middle of the corral. For us first-timers, there was a bench by the fence that we could stand on, and the counselors would help us get on our horses.

They had a big platform so Bill could get on his massive horse. But before he even started to climb up on the platform, Bill called out, "Stop! Wait! Don't get on that horse!"

We all wondered who he was yelling at, but then Bill went running on all fours to the middle of the corral. Caroline was on the right side of her horse, getting ready to mount up.

Bill tried to stop before he got to her, but he didn't slow down quickly enough, and ended up giving Caroline a light push with his tusks (not the pointy parts). She fell on the ground.

"I'm terribly sorry," Bill said. "It's just, well, we should go talk to Wrangler Scott. Are you all right?"

"I'm fine," Caroline said. "But we sure are going to talk to the Wrangler! I've never seen such behavior."

Caroline and Bill went to talk to the Wrangler. First, Bill talked to Wrangler Scott. Then, Wrangler Scott talked to Caroline.

I saw the Wrangler patting Bill on the back. He went and got Caroline another horse.

Luke ended up riding Wild Fire, who reared up on his hind legs, but eventually calmed down.

We had a good ride. Most of us went slowly on a path. The more experienced riders got to gallop, but us "Sweetfoots" kept a slower pace. I noticed Caroline didn't gallop her horse.

Later I asked Bill, "What happened with Caroline?"

"I saw that she wasn't qualified to ride Wild Fire and might be in danger if she rode him," Bill said. "I think she was just trying to impress Luke. Fortunately, Wrangler Scott agreed."

"But how did you know that?" I asked.

"Don't worry about it, Sweetfoot," Bill said. "Sometimes you humans take foolish chances for the opposite sex, but I guess God knew what He was doing on the sixth day."

How did Bill know that Caroline shouldn't be riding Wild Fire? And what did God do on the sixth day?

 Turn to page 104 to find out!

Chapter 8

The Case of the Big Nap

It was the last full of day of camp, and frankly, I was starting to feel pretty tired. I had been busy every day from early in the morning until late at night, and I hadn't been getting a lot of sleep.

So, after breakfast and Sunday morning church service, I was happy to play word puzzles with Bill in the rec room. Bill has a much bigger vocabulary than I do, so he lets me make up words to make it even. A fake word only counts if it makes Bill laugh.

I was still losing the game pretty badly, so I didn't mind when Mike interrupted to show us his new *Phil the Warthog* comic.

"So does this one tell how Phil escapes from Dr.

Werner von Doomcough on the spaceship?" I asked.

"No," Mike said. "I can't finish that storyline until I get a chance to research orbital reentry, so I've started a different Phil story. Would you guys like to look at it?"

"Definitely," I said, if only to get away from my humiliating word puzzle defeat.

This comic opened with Phil at a briefing with a dozen other agents, all human. Shady Thomkins was giving a presentation on a massive computer screen:

••

"So," Shady said, "we know that Dr. Werner von Doomcough has built this enormous ray off the coast. He's planning to aim it at the mainland, but we have no idea what that beam is meant to do.

"Unfortunately," Shady continued, "the island is not in our jurisdiction or area of responsibility, so we can't investigate there."

As Shady spoke, all the agents except for Phil were yawning. Soon, Shady was yawning as well. "Okay," Shady said, "I want you all out on the streets investigating this. I want to know what the bad Doctor is up to this time."

Everyone was assigned a different region to

investigate. Phil was sent to the mean streets of downtown Azusa.

It wasn't long before Phil noticed something odd was going on.

On every corner, Phil saw street vendors calling out the same thing: "Warm milk! Get your free warm milk! Get your free warm milk here!"

Then Phil saw something else extraordinary. A plane flying overhead was dropping something to the ground, but it didn't seem to be dropping anything dangerous. Soon there were blankets all over the ground. Not ordinary blankets, but small, soft, well-worn blankets. Phil thought he would even go so far as to call them "blankies."

Then, something even more bizarre happened. Phil saw a little girl wearing sunglasses and a helmet coming down the street. She was carrying a shepherd's staff and was leading a large flock of sheep.

Phil noticed that many people on the street had taken the warm milk, picked up a blanket, and were counting the sheep as they passed by. Soon, all the people seemed to be lying down for a nap. Everyone that had been driving a car or truck had pulled over to the side of the road for a nap as well.

Phil went right over to his cell phone and called Shady Thomkins.

"Shady," Phil said, "I have to tell you about this most amazing thing I'm witnessing!"

Phil heard Shady respond, "Huh, what?" and then Phil heard the sound of Shady Thomkins snoring.

Phil looked in the window of an appliance store, where several networks were broadcasting on large screen TVs. The usual shows had been interrupted for a news bulletin, but the news anchors had fallen asleep—sound asleep.

Phil knew it was up to him to investigate this strange phenomenon. To do it, he was going to have to go to Doomcough's island. Fortunately, he had a special amphibious government vehicle that was able to travel across the land and sea very quickly.

Phil landed on a remote part of the island and got out of his vehicle to look around. Marching around the island were guards wearing helmets like the one the shepherd girl had been wearing. Phil kicked himself for not having talked to

her. (It's easier to kick yourself when you have four legs instead of two.)

Phil was able to sneak past the guards and into a building topped by a giant ray. He made his way through the hallways to the control room of the ray itself. Phil saw walls covered with lights, dials, and switches. One of the walls had a series of monitors for the security cameras posted throughout the building. Anyone in this room should have seen Phil coming.

But the only person Phil saw in the room was a man stretched out on his back in the middle of the floor. Phil almost wondered if the man was alive. He was very still, not breathing heavily, and his closed eyes were very still.

Phil nudged the man with his tusks.

"Oh, you woke me," the man said. "And I was just in the middle of an amazing dream."

"I'm Phil the Warthog, government agent," Phil said. "Tell me who you are and about that dream."

"My name is Nemo Sanders," the man said as he stretched. "And I was dreaming that Dr. Werner von Doomcough had built a ray to broadcast a very powerful lullaby to put everyone to sleep so that he could go on a crime spree."

"You were dreaming that?" Phil asked.

"Actually, as you woke me," Nemo said, "I was dreaming I was surrounded by a herd of pink elephants, but I dreamed the other things earlier."

"I don't believe you were asleep," Phil said. "And I certainly don't believe you were just dreaming. I think you said that so I would doubt you were working with Dr. Doomcough. Now tell me what you were really doing just now!"

● ●

"That's all I have so far," Mike said.

"Hey, I figured out something," I said. "I bet those helmets keep people from falling asleep, and warthogs are immune to the ray. But why didn't Phil believe that Nemo had been dreaming?"

"That's obvious," Bill said. "I can't believe you can't dream up the answer. But this story has reminded me about something important about the seventh day. I'm going to go to the cabin and take a nap!"

Why didn't Phil believe that Nemo had been dreaming? And what does the seventh day have to do with naps?

 Turn to page 106 to find out!

Chapter 9

The Case of the Diamondback

The last evening of camp, after we ate dinner and the plates were cleared, Mr. Wayne went to the front of the room and announced that they were going to show some film clips and a slideshow from the week at camp.

They had some video clips of Bill waterskiing, horseback riding, and rappelling off a boulder. Whenever people saw Bill on the screen, they let out a big cheer. (I think if you look in the right place, you can find some of those images on the Internet.)

There were also a lot of nature shots, including many pictures of wildlife. When they showed a picture of a snake, Ethan let out a big scream. A lot of kids laughed, and others pointed at Ethan. Bill told me later that he noticed Chris Franklin sneak out of the building a little after that.

After the show, Mr. Wayne went up to the front and gave a talk.

"As you know, Scouting isn't sponsored by churches, so we don't talk about religion. But the Scouts do have God as part of their motto, so I'd like to talk a bit about the world that God made."

Mr. Wayne then went on to talk about the "ecosystem" of the land around the camp and how the plants and animals were all part of a system that worked together. He said he believed that the beauty of nature and the way things worked together showed that there was a Creator—that things came together through design, not random chance.

"Even mosquitoes have a place," he said. "We might think of them as a nuisance, but even they have a place in God's design. Did you know mosquitoes help deer and other animals migrate at the best time?"

He went on to talk about snakes and their place in the ecosystem. He showed a lot of pictures of snakes.

I noticed some guys were whispering and giggling and pointing at Ethan. Ethan was covering his eyes.

Then some kids started teasing him, "Hey Ethan, is the little girl afraid of the big, bad snake?" It went on like that. Eventually Ethan hobbled out of the room.

He said he was going to the bathroom, but we saw him leave the building.

"I've got a bad feeling about this," Bill said. "Let's follow him."

We kept our distance, but we watched Ethan with his bad foot make his way up toward his cabin.

We saw the light go on in his cabin, and then we heard a scream. Bill and I turned to each other and ran full speed up the hill.

Ethan stood frozen in the doorway. We looked past him to see a snake on his bunk.

Then, we heard the sound of laughter. Chris Franklin was behind us, laughing so hard he was snorting.

"That was the funniest thing I've ever heard," he said. "You scream like a girl."

Bill was not laughing. "Get out of the doorway, Ethan," Bill said. "Move back."

Bill looked more grim than he had when the bear was in Chris' cabin.

"Nick," Bill said. "Did you notice the dark, diamond markings on the back of the snake?"

"Yeah," I said. "What about it?"

"Have you ever heard of diamondbacks?" he said.

"You mean diamondback rattlesnakes?" I said. "But it doesn't have a rattle."

"Sometimes snakes have accidents, get hurt, and lose their rattles," he said. "I think that's what we're dealing with. Go with Chris and Ethan into our cabin."

"Go into my cabin, guys," I said, still standing in the doorway behind Bill. "I'm not leaving, Bill. You might need help."

"Okay," Bill said. "Thanks. But stand back."

Bill walked slowly into the cabin. He picked up a suitcase with his mouth and held it in front of him.

The snake coiled up, ready to spring.

Bill kept moving forward.

The snake sprang, and Bill hid behind the case.

The snake struck the case and then hit the floor. It seemed a bit stunned.

Bill took the opportunity and scooped up the snake up with his tusks. He began to toss it up and catch it with his tusks as he headed out the door.

Bill took the snake far into the woods and left it.

"I'll alert Mr. Wayne," Bill said. "I hope the snake doesn't return. If it does, it may have to be destroyed."

Chris and Ethan had walked back from the other cabin. "Don't tell Mr. Wayne," Chris said. "I don't need to get into more trouble. They'll never let me come back here again."

"You should have thought about that before you pulled this little stunt," Bill said.

"I just noticed during the slideshow that Ethan was afraid of snakes," Chris said. "You have to admit it was funny when he screamed."

"Yeah right. It'd have been real funny if I'd been bitten by a rattlesnake," Ethan said.

"But it didn't have a rattle. How was I supposed to know? I saw the snake under the cabin, and I used a stick to carry it to your cabin," Chris said. "I know about snakes. I know which ones are poisonous. I even know that rhyme...

'Red and yellow, it's a nice fellow,

Red and black, get back, Jack!'"

"As if I needed more proof of how little you know!" Bill said. "You've proved you know nothing about snakes, especially that first serpent. This is the last straw, Chris. You are going to have to change."

Then I saw something I never thought I would see. I saw tears in Chris Franklin's eyes. I guess he didn't want us to see that, because he took off running into the woods.

What extra proof did Bill have to show him that Chris didn't know about snakes? And who was the "first serpent" that Bill was talking about?

 Turn to page 108 to find out!

Chapter 10

The Case of
the Missing Camper

It wasn't long before other campers joined us near the cabins. Mr. Fonda asked what had happened, and Bill told him.

"Everyone to your cabins," Mr. Fonda called.

"Can Nick and I wait here for Chris to come back?" Bill asked.

"I suppose so," Mr. Fonda said. "I take it you're friends back home?"

"We certainly have spent a lot of time together," Bill said.

Mr. Stewart and Mr. Wayne had gone searching for Chris, but after about an hour they came back.

"Did Chris return?" Mr. Stewart asked.

"No," I responded.

It was approaching midnight. Counselors searched the camp for another hour, but they didn't find Chris.

"Excuse me, Mr. Fonda," Bill asked. "Could I help look for Chris? I'm a decent tracker."

"We're not on the African savanna," Mr. Fonda said. "You don't know these mountains."

"Chris doesn't know them either," Bill said. "I think I can help."

"I suppose you can go," Mr. Fonda said, "as long as you stay with Mr. Stewart and do what he says."

Mr. Stewart and I had flashlights, but Bill said he didn't need one. We walked in the direction Chris had run. In the woods, Bill got down on all fours and sniffed the ground.

"I've got a trace," Bill said. "Nick, shine the flashlight in front of my nose. Can you see the tracks from Chris' tennis shoe?"

I could and so could Mr. Stewart. We continued searching with Bill sniffing the ground and occasionally pointing out a clear track or a broken twig. It was getting cool, so I was glad Mr. Stewart had insisted that I put on a sweatshirt. I figured Chris must be getting chilly.

We came to a rocky patch. Bill wasn't finding any more footprints, but he said the scent was still strong.

"Does your tribe use scent to track water buffalo or some such thing?" Mr. Stewart asked at one point.

"This is just the most basic kind of detective work," Bill replied.

Along the way we kept calling out to Chris, but we got no answer. Then we came across a smell that even my nose couldn't miss: skunk.

"It looks like Chris ran into something he wasn't expecting," Bill said.

Bill pointed to more tennis shoe tracks on the ground, and then to tracks that I didn't recognize. "That's skunk," Bill said. "I think Chris got sprayed."

We followed the tennis shoe tracks, and I think even I could have tracked Chris by smell now. We called out again, and this time we could hear a faint response. We started to run.

We found Chris huddled in the bottom of a big burned-out tree.

"Warthog…I mean, Bill," Chris said, trying to stand up quickly. He was stiff, so it took time. Then he held out his hand to shake Bill's hoof. "I thought if anyone could find me, it would be you. Thanks."

I would have been a little less surprised if we had tracked down the skunk, and it had held out its paw and said, "Thanks."

"Thank you too, Nick," Chris said. "And Mr. Stewart. I might have been stuck out here for a long time if you hadn't looked for me."

Walking back to camp, we were all pretty quiet. Mr. Stewart asked Chris why he had run.

He said, "I don't know. I knew I couldn't talk myself out of this one. And there were so many people I felt like I needed to apologize to. And when I was out here, I started thinking about what Mr. Wayne said tonight about when you look around, you have to know there's a God. And suddenly I felt like I needed to say sorry to Him somehow. But I really didn't know how to do that."

"Maybe we can talk about that on the ride home," I said. "Want to ride in our van?"

"Yeah," Chris said. "If you guys don't mind."

"I think it would be alright," Bill said. "But asking the other kids might be in odor, I mean order."

"I'll check the kitchen for tomato juice," Mr. Stewart said.

"I believe that's a myth," Bill said. "But at least the windows of the van will be down."

I'll be honest here: I didn't know what Bill and Mr. Stewart were talking about, but we were soon back at camp.

On the drive back home, almost everyone rode in the front seats of the van. Chris and I rode in the very back seat. All the windows were down, but everyone used the clothespins that Bill borrowed from the camp laundry, including Chris and me.

I'd like to be able to tell you that from that day forward, Chris was always a great guy. But he wasn't.

He was, though, a better guy.

Bill says there is an old saying when it comes to detective stories, "The butler did it." I guess it's because there were a lot of mysteries that all ended with the butler being the bad guy.

It used to be that the solution to a whole lot of Bill's cases was, "Chris did it." But from that day forward, that wasn't always the case.

Bill told Chris that in the beginning, God made a lot of different creations. Bill told Chris that God is still making new creations. And I think Chris finally realized that Bill knew what he was talking about.

Why was Mr. Stewart talking about tomato juice? And what did Bill mean when he said God is still making "new creations"?

 Turn to page 110 to find out!

The Case of the Veering Van

Q: *How did Bill know that Chris wasn't telling the truth?*

A: Chris said he saw the letters "Q through Z" on a license plate. That would be ten letters!

Most license plates have a mix of numbers and letters, except vanity plates that allow people to choose what goes on their plate. But even then, there are never more than seven numbers or letters on the plate. Chris had started off his story, and the week at camp, with a lie.

Q: *What did Bill mean when he referred to "the very beginning?"*

A: Bill was encouraging Chris to spend the week considering the very beginning, when God created the world and everything in it. You can find out about the very beginning of everything

92

at the beginning of the Bible, in the first chapters of the book of Genesis.

As for whether Chris will have a new beginning, we'll have to wait to find out.

One other thing: remember that license plates can only have a combination of up to seven numbers and letters? Well, it just so happens, seven is an important number in this book—and I'm not talking about the seven s'mores Nick ate on campfire night that made his stomach queasy.

The Case of the Sticky Doorknobs

Q: *How did Bill and Mr. Wayne know that Chris wasn't telling the truth?*

A: Bill and Mr. Wayne knew that Chris wasn't telling the truth because of the "light" touch he added to his story.

Chris' cabin was uphill and east from Nick's cabin. To look toward Nick's cabin, he would be facing west. Therefore, the sun, which rises in the east, could not be in his eyes.

Ethan needed three stitches. He got the stitches from Mrs. Wayne and an apology from Chris. Chris was also assigned clean-up duty after dinner for the rest of the week.

Q: *What did Bill mean about it being "fitting that on the first day, we should shed some light on Chris' character?"*

A: Bill was thinking of the story of creation in the Bible. Genesis 1:3 describes the First Day of creation in this way, "And God said, 'Let there be light,' and there was light."

God is still bringing light into our lives. Every morning when the sun rises, it is a gift from God. And He brings light to us in other ways.

In John 8:12 Jesus said, "I am the light of the world." We need His light every day, just as much as we need the sunlight.

The Case of the Waterskiing Warthog

Q: *Why didn't Bill believe Ethan story about barefoot waterskiing?*

A: Well, first of all, Bill knew that people who brag about themselves often make things up. This is especially true of people who are trying to impress people they have just met.

But the waterskiing story had another problem. Ethan said the speedometer read 100 MPH. The problem is that sailboats usually only travel 5-10 MPH, and the world record, set by a sailboat specifically designed for racing, is about 62 MPH.

So Bill knew Ethan's family's sailboat couldn't possibly go 100 MPH, which cast doubt on that story from Ethan—and all his other stories.

Q: *Why was Bill thankful for the second day?*

A: Genesis 1:6-9 tells about God separating the waters from the sky on the second day.

Water is cool stuff. Not only do we need to drink it to live, but as Nick, Mike, and Bill were reminded in the boat, it's pretty fun to play in, too.

In John 4:14, Jesus tells about water He gives that brings eternal life. That's sure better than anything you'll find in a lake or bottled on your grocery store shelf.

The Case of the Poison Oak Sandwich

Q: *How did Bill know that Ethan wasn't telling the truth?*

A: Bill had been pretty sure of his ability to identify poison oak, but he was even more certain that Ethan wasn't an expert on plant life.

Ethan said his father had pointed out poison oak in the Rocky and Appalachian Mountains, but poison oak can be found only in the Pacific Coast states and some places on the Atlantic Coast. Poison ivy can be found in most other parts of the United States.

Ethan wanted to impress Bill and Nick with his stories, but he finally realized that it wasn't the best way to make friends. People wanted to make friends with the real Ethan.

Q: *Why did Bill say that it was appropriate to veg out on the third day?*

A: In the book of Genesis, land was formed and produced vegetation on the Third Day. Genesis 1:11 says, "God said, 'Let the land produce vegetation: seed-bearing plants and trees on the land that bear fruit with seed in it, according to their various kinds.' And it was so."

God is concerned about plants growing, but He's more concerned about our growing close to Him.

The Case of the Meteor Bath

Q: *How did Phil know the man was lying?*

A: The man had said he heard "a cry for help from outside the ship," but sound doesn't travel in the vacuum of space. He couldn't have heard the man in the spacesuit. He must have been watching for someone he was working with.

(Spoiler alert: If you don't happen to see the next issue of *Phil the Warthog*, don't worry. Phil does save the world from the bombarding bathtubs.)

Q: *What does the fourth day have to do with a meteor shower?*

A: Genesis 1:14 describes what happened on the Fourth Day. "And God said, 'Let there be lights in the expanse of the sky to separate the day from the night, and let them serve as signs to mark seasons and days and years.'"

This verse can be confusing if it means the stars and sun and moon were made after the Earth was made. Genesis 1:1 already said, "In the beginning God created the heavens and the Earth."

People have tried to explain this puzzler in various ways including: 1) The heavens couldn't be seen from the land until God let them be seen on the Fourth Day. 2) The chapter is written in a poetic way, and so it is restating what was mentioned in the first verse. 3) God is declaring people will use the skies to mark time.

There is still a lot of mystery about how God created the world. But we can trust He knew what He was doing.

The Case of the Snacking Bear

Q: *How did Bill convince Mr. Fonda that Chris was lying?*

A: It wasn't Bill's knowledge of bears, but of raccoons that cast doubt on Chris' story. Chris said that the raccoons raided the dog food and the garbage while he was at school.

Raccoons are primarily nocturnal animals, meaning they're usually out scavenging at night. And Bill knew Chris didn't go to night school. Bill convinced Mr. Fonda that Chris made up the story to cover up the fact that he had brought the food into the cabin.

Q: *Why did Bill say that it would be more appropriate to talk about animals on the sixth day of camp?*

A: Genesis 1:20–25 tells of God creating living things—the birds of the sky, the creatures of the sea, and the land animals. The birds and sea animals were created on the fifth day, and the land animals and people on the sixth.

Aren't you glad that God gave us the company of animals? He gave us everything from our dogs and cats to the duckbilled platypus and the pintail snipe. You can't say God doesn't have an imagination!

The Case of the Confident Cowgirl

Q: *How did Bill know that Caroline shouldn't be riding Wild Fire?*

A: Bill had noticed that Caroline seemed to like Luke and must have wanted to impress him with her stories of riding horses in shows. But Bill knew there was a real problem when he saw Caroline trying to mount the horse from the right side. It is customary for riders to mount the horse on the left side. That is what trained horses will expect.

Bill knew that Caroline wasn't really an experienced rider and that she would be in danger riding Wild Fire.

Q: *What did God do on the sixth day?*

A: A lot! Genesis 1:24-31 tells of God making the animals of the land and man and woman. Genesis 1:27 says, "So God created man in his own image, in the image of God he created him; male and female he created them."

It's a fact that there comes a time in life when girls try to impress boys and boys try to impress girls. But it's important to remember that it's most important to please God, and we should do all we do with Him in mind.

The Case of the Big Nap

Q: *Why didn't Phil believe that Nemo had really been dreaming?*

A: Nemo had been on the floor very still. Phil noticed that his eyes were very still, but when people dream in their sleep, their eyes move beneath their lids. It's called Rapid Eye Movement (REM).

So Phil knew Nemo was pretending he had fallen under the sleep ray's lullaby spell, when he was, in fact, working with Dr. Werner von Doomcough.

Q: *What does the seventh day have to do with rest?*
A: Genesis 2:2-3 says,

"By the seventh day God had finished the work he had been doing; so on the seventh day he rested from all his work. And God blessed the seventh day and made it holy, because on it he rested from all the work of creating that he had done."

God knew that rest was very important for us, so He set the example Himself.

So when your parents talk about bedtimes and the importance of sleep, realize that they know what they're talking about. Just don't try to nap in the streets of Azusa. That only works in the comics.

The Case of the Diamondback

Q: *What extra proof did Bill have to show him that Chris didn't know about snakes?*

A: Bill knew Chris had been dabbling in dangerous matters he knew nothing about when Chris said he thought the rattle was the only way to tell a rattlesnake. He hadn't bothered to look at the snake's markings.

But even worse, he got the venomous snake rhyme (which warns of coral snakes) wrong. It really goes, "Red and yellow, kills a fellow. Red and black is safe for Jack."

Q: *Who was the "first serpent" that Bill was talking about?*

A: As for the first serpent (or snake), Bill was referring to the creature in Genesis 3 who tempted Eve (who then tempted Adam) to disobey

108

God and eat the fruit God had forbidden. That was the first sin.

Bill had seen Chris do a lot of things that were wrong. But this practical joke could have gotten someone badly hurt, perhaps killed. He let Chris know how serious sin can be.

As to whether Chris finally took sin seriously, you'll have to read the next chapter.

Q: *Where should a person look on the internet for snapshots of Bill at Camp?*

A: Sorry, but telling you the secret website address, (which happens to be www.CheeseWaddles.com) would take all the adventure out of your search!

The Case of the Missing Camper

Q: *Why was Mr. Stewart talking about tomato juice?*

A: A topic on everyone's mind, even if they didn't want to hurt Chris' feelings by saying it out loud, was how bad the skunk spray on Chris would smell on the drive home.

Some people believe that tomato juice gets rid of the smell of skunk, but as Bill said, that's just a myth. There is no scientific evidence that it works. Chris took a long shower at Bill's suggestion and applied a baking soda solution.

The shower helped, but Chris still had a pretty potent odor on the ride home. Nick still stuck with him, though, because Chris wanted to know how to say he was sorry to God.

![TOMATO JUICE]

Q: *What did Bill mean when he said God is still making "new creations?"*

A: Nick explained we've all done things wrong—hitting other kids, lying, disobeying our parents and teachers. And since God made everyone, when we do rotten things to other people, it's like we are doing them to God.

As the Bible says in 1 John 1:9, "If we confess our sins, he (God) is faithful and just and will forgive us our sins and purify us from all unrighteousness." Nick told Chris that the cost for the things we've done wrong was paid for when Jesus, God's Son, died on the cross.

That's what Bill was talking about when he said God is still making new creations. 2 Corinthians 5:17 says, "Therefore, if anyone is in Christ, he is a new creation."

Chris became a new person in Christ. You can be one too. You just have to ask Him.

God never stops creating new, really cool stuff... and people.

More fun devotionals that help you grow closer to God.

Gotta Have God (for guys) and *God and Me!* (for girls) are packed with over 100 devotionals, plus memory verses, stories, journal space and fun activities to help you learn more about the Bible.

Gotta Have God for Guys 10-12, Vol. 1
ISBN 1-885358-98-9

Gotta Have God for Guys 10-12, Vol. 2
ISBN 1-58411-059-7

God and Me! for Girls 10-12, Vol. 1
ISBN 1-885358-54-7

God and Me! for Girls 10-12, Vol. 2
ISBN 1-58411-056-2

Visit www.LegacyPressKids.com for more great stuff!